Helen Orme taught for many years before giving up teaching to write full-time. At the last count she had written over 70 books.

She writes both fiction and non-fiction, but at present is concentrating on fiction for older readers.

Helen also runs writing workshops for children and courses for teachers in both primary and secondary schools.

How many have you read?

Wet!

Helen Orme

Ransom

JF / ORM (Fast Fiction)

P 00096

Wet!

by Helen Orme
Illustrated by Cathy Brett
Cover by Anna Torborg

Published by Ransom Publishing Ltd.
51 Southgate Street, Winchester, Hants. SO23 9EH
www.ransom.co.uk

ISBN   978 184167 688 3

First published in 2007

Meet the Sisters ...

Siti and her friends are really close. So close she calls them her Sisters. They've been mates for ever, and most of the time they are closer than her real family.

Siti is the leader – the one who always knows what to do – but Kelly, Lu, Donna and Rachel have their own lives to lead as well.

Still, there's no one you can talk to, no one you can rely on, like your best mates. Right?

1

Much too early!

It was very early in the morning. Too early! Lu's dad was dropping her and Kelly off at school.

"Have a good time, girls," he said. "Ring when you get there!"

"Come on everyone, get on the coach," said Mr Jackson.

Kelly and Lu settled down in their seats. They were going to Wales on a camping trip. They were staying two nights and were going rock climbing. It was activities week at school and they had spent two days training. Now it was going to be the real thing.

Lu looked round at the boys sitting behind them.

"Look, it's Joel and Dan."

"Dan's not bad, but Joel thinks a lot of himself," said Kelly. "I wish Gary and Simon were on the trip instead."

"I'm glad they're not," said Lu, "or you'd be falling down all the rocks trying to look for Gary."

Kelly laughed. "You could be right."

Halfway there, the rain started. Soon it was chucking it down.

"Good job we haven't got to put up the tents ourselves," said Kelly.

It was still pouring when they arrived at the campsite. They had to stay on the coach while the teachers told them what to do and where to go.

They went to put their gear in their tents.

Lu looked at their tent in horror.

"What on Earth is this?"

"It's a tent – what do you think it is?" said Kelly.

"It's not a tent – it's a disaster," said Lu. "I thought it was going to be one of those big ones with a window and a proper door and things."

2

Team–building

Just then, Michelle and Chris arrived. They were sharing with Kelly and Lu.

"Haven't you ever been in a tent before?" said Michelle.

"Yeah," said Lu, "in France. The tents are big and comfortable and have loads of stuff in them."

"This is a school camp," said Chris. "Things don't work like that in school camps!"

They pushed open the tent flap and went in. There wasn't much room, just about enough space for the four beds.

They dumped their bags and went off to the meal tent. At least that was big and it was warmer.

Later, they were told the plans for the next day. They were put into teams. The four girls would be in the same team as Joel and Dan. Lu was pleased. In spite of Kelly's comments about Joel, she still quite fancied him.

The evening was fun. They were doing 'team-building exercises' – which meant that they had to get into their groups and do silly things.

"I'm not going to eat grubs for anybody!" said Michelle.

"You're alright – you're not a celebrity!" said Chris.

It was still raining when they went back to their tent.

Lu got into her sleeping bag.

"It's cold," she moaned.

"Put your sweater on," said Chris.

Lu got out again. She put on her sweater, her socks and her woolly hat!

Kelly laughed, but then she put on her socks, too.

Everything was fine until the next morning. Chris got out of bed – and screamed!

3

Bad news

The other three sat up.

"Spiders!" shrieked Michelle, who hated spiders.

"What's going on?" demanded Kelly.

"There's a river in the tent!" screeched Chris, jumping back onto her bed.

The bed wasn't meant to be jumped on. It collapsed into the big puddle. That made Chris scream even more.

The tent flap opened and Miss Harper looked in.

"Whatever is going on?" she asked. "We can hear you all over the camp."

Chris pointed at the puddle.

"You're not the only ones," said Miss Harper. "It's been raining all night. Chris, bring your sleeping bag to me when you're dressed, and I'll get it dried."

They got dressed sitting on their beds and Chris went off with her bag. She came back with a bucket and some cloths.

"We need to be quick," she said. "There's a meeting after breakfast."

It was bad news. Because of all the rain they had decided it wouldn't be safe to go climbing.

"It's not all bad news," said Mr Jackson. "We are going to set up an orienteering course instead. You have to work round a course through the woods, using your map-reading skills. It's quite a challenge."

"I don't want to go plodding through soggy woods," moaned Lu. "I want to go rock climbing."

"Come on," said Kelly. "It will be O.K., and we'll be with Joel and Dan all day."

But Lu didn't want to be cheered up. She didn't like being cold and she hated being wet.

4

"Don't do anything silly"

The teams were ready. They were given maps, compasses and food and drink. There were lots of checkpoints around the course.

"Now remember, you're not racing each other," said Mr Jackson. "Don't do anything silly."

Miss Harper handed out whistles.

"If you get into trouble, just blow this and someone will come and get you," she said.

They set off up a steep slope.

"Shouldn't we look at the map first and decide on the best way?" said Michelle.

"No worries," said Joel. "We've had a quick look. Just follow us, girlies, and you'll be O.K."

"Don't call us girlies," said Chris.

Joel grinned at Dan. He knew just what would wind her up.

The boys pushed their way to the front.

"Keep up!" called Dan, as he pushed past Michelle.

The four girls looked at each other.

"We're going to have to do something about them!" said Chris.

They soon got to the first checkpoint. The boys were way ahead and had already had their drinks.

"Come on, come on," said Joel. "We've got to go faster."

5

Teaching them a lesson

Michelle looked at Lu.

"Just give us a minute to look at the map," she said to Joel.

"Look," she said to Lu. "If we let them get ahead, we can cut through this way and get ahead of them."

"We can't do that," said Lu. "We're supposed to stay together. Anyway, I don't care. I'm fed up. I hate this! I wanted to go climbing."

Michelle glared at Lu.

"You're hopeless!"

She called to Chris. "Over here, come on."

Chris and Kelly ran over. Michelle explained her plan.

"Come on," shouted Joel again.

"Come on," said Michelle. She looked at Lu and Kelly. "You do what you want – *we're* going to teach those two a lesson."

She started running. Chris shrugged, and followed Michelle.

"What are we going to do?" asked Lu. "We've got to go with one lot."

"Better stick with the boys. At least they're following the right path."

They set off, running to try to catch up. Lu was still moaning, and to make things worse it had started to rain again.

The boys were just about in sight. Joel looked back.

"It's O.K.," he said to Dan, "they're following us. I can see two of them."

They got to a point where the path split. One way went on up the hillside, the other went down.

"We carry on up here," said Dan. Joel looked back.

"Can't see the girls – we'd better wait a bit."

The rain was getting heavier and they couldn't see anything.

Then there was a scream!

6

A horrible crunch

"It came from down there!" Joel pointed down the other path.

He leapt down the bank – and started to slide.

The path had turned into a river of mud and Joel couldn't stop himself. He slid faster and faster.

There was a horrible crunch as he got caught up by a tree trunk.

Dan followed – carefully. He could see Joel lying very, very still.

"Hey," he yelled. "Who's there? Where are you? What's happened?"

Now everything was quiet. Too quiet!

Dan got to Joel. He was lying against the tree trunk. His head was bleeding.

Dan yelled again. "Help!"

He heard giggling as, through the rain, Chris and Michelle appeared, struggling up the slippy path.

"Fooled you!" called Chris.

Then Michelle saw Joel. She screamed again. This time for real.

"What's going on?" A voice came from above. Kelly was peering down at them.

"It's Joel – he's hurt."

"What are we going to do?" Chris was beginning to panic.

Michelle started to tug at Joel. "Come on, stop messing about."

Lu arrived beside them.

"Stop that," she ordered. "We mustn't move him. Who's got the whistle?"

"Me," said Dan, fishing it out from his pocket.

"Give it to Chris. Now – you go back up to Kelly and the two of you get to the next checkpoint."

"Chris," she turned to the other girl. "Keep blowing the whistle."

Lu had forgotten all about the rain and cold. She was too worried about Joel. She took off her coat and put it over him. Now all she had to do was wait.

Luckily, they were close to the checkpoint. By the time Mr Jackson arrived, Lu was soaked, but Joel had opened his eyes. Lu wouldn't let him move, but she kept talking to him.